Percy's Surprise!

Illustrated by Peter Lawson
Series Editor: Teresa Wilson

Thomas the Tank Engine & Friends

A BRITT ALLCROFT COMPANY PRODUCTION

Based on The Railway Series by The Rev W Awdry

© Gullane (Thomas) LLC 2003

All rights reserved
Published in Great Britain in 2003 by Egmont Books Limited,
239 Kensington High Street, London, W8 6SA
Printed in China
ISBN 0 7498 5752 8

10 9 8 7 6 5 4 3 2 1

Educational consultant: Nicola Morgan, literacy expert and author of over 60 early learning books.

Percy was behaving very oddly.

He was whispering to his driver.

"What are you doing?" asked Henry.

"It's a surprise," said Percy.

"You'll have to wait."

"What are they doing?" asked Thomas.

"What is that square for, Henry?"

"It's a surprise," said Henry.

"You'll have to wait."

"What is Percy doing?"
asked James.

"What is that cube for,
Thomas?"

"It's a surprise," said Thomas.

"You'll have to wait."

"What are they doing?" asked Edward.

"What are those circles for, James?"

"It's a surprise," said James.

"You'll have to wait."

All of a sudden, The Fat Controller appeared.

"What are you doing?" he said.

"What is that cone for?"

"It's a surprise!" said Percy.

"You'll have to wait."

Then the shed doors shut.

Percy stayed in the shed for a long time.

The trains waited.

And waited.

Even The Fat Controller waited.

At last the shed door opened.

Percy's driver said, "You can look now. Look at what Percy has made."

All the trains thought that Percy was very clever.

"But where's the cone, Percy?" they asked.

"On my head!" laughed Percy.